GREAT WHITE
SHARK
ADVENTURE

FABIEN COUSTEAU
EXPEDITIONS

GREAT WHITE
SHARK
ADVENTURE

WRITTEN BY

JAMES O. FRAIOLI

ILLUSTRATED BY

JOE ST.PIERRE

MARGARET K. McELDERRY BOOKS

NEW YORK   LONDON   TORONTO   SYDNEY   NEW DELHI

AUTHORS' NOTE

Great White Shark Adventure is a work of fiction
based on actual expeditions and accepted ideas
about the ocean and its inhabitants.

MARGARET K. McELDERRY BOOKS
An imprint of Simon & Schuster Children's Publishing Division
1230 Avenue of the Americas, New York, New York 10020
This book is a work of fiction. Any references to historical events, real people,
or real places are used fictitiously. Other names, characters, places, and events
are products of the author's imagination, and any resemblance to actual
events or places or persons, living or dead, is entirely coincidental.
Text copyright © 2019 by James O. Fraioli and Fabien Cousteau
Illustrations copyright © 2019 by Joseph St.Pierre
All rights reserved, including the right of reproduction in whole or in part in any form.
MARGARET K. McELDERRY BOOKS is a trademark of Simon & Schuster, Inc.
For information about special discounts for bulk purchases, please contact Simon & Schuster
Special Sales at 1-866-506-1949 or business@simonandschuster.com.
The Simon & Schuster Speakers Bureau can bring authors to your live event.
For more information or to book an event, contact the Simon & Schuster Speakers
Bureau at 1-866-248-3049 or visit our website at www.simonspeakers.com.
Book design by Sonia Chaghatzbanian
The text for this book was set in Chaparral Pro.
The illustrations for this book were rendered digitally.
Manufactured in China
1218 SCP
First Edition
10 9 8 7 6 5 4 3 2 1
Library of Congress Cataloging-in-Publication Data
Names: Fraioli, James O. (Cookbook author), author. | St.Pierre, Joe, illustrator. |
Cousteau, Fabien.
Title: Great white shark adventure/ written by James Fraioli ; illustrated by Joe St.Pierre.
Description: First edition. | New York : Margaret K. McElderry Books, [2019] |
Series: Fabien Cousteau expeditions ; 1 | Summary: Bella, twelve, and Marcus, thirteen,
join Fabien Cousteau's research team off the coast of South Africa as they try to find and
tag an extraordinarily large great white shark. Inserts include facts about sharks and other
marine animals, equipment used by researchers studying sharks, and more.
Identifiers: LCCN 2017049313 (print) | ISBN 9781534420878 (paper-over-board) |
ISBN 9781534420885 (hardcover) | ISBN 9781534420892 (eBook)
Subjects: | CYAC: White shark—Fiction. | Sharks—Fiction. | Wildlife conservation—
Fiction. | Cousteau, Fabien, Fiction. | Scientists—Fiction. | Marine animals—Fiction.
Classification: LCC PZ7.1.F715 Gre 2019 (print) | DDC [Fic]—dc23
LC record available at https://lccn.loc.gov/2017049313

GREAT WHITE
SHARK
ADVENTURE

AUGUST 4,
6:07 AM

MANY PEOPLE EAT TUNA FISH.

FOR THOSE WHO ENJOY TUNA, IT'S BEST TO SELECT TUNA CAUGHT USING POLE-AND-LINE (A TRADITIONAL FISHING METHOD IN WHICH TUNA ARE CAUGHT ONE FISH AT A TIME).

THIS IS A MUCH BETTER ALTERNATIVE THAN TUNA CAUGHT USING LONG-LINES, IN WHICH THOUSANDS OF BAITED HOOKS ARE SET FOR MILES IN THE OCEAN.

THIS LEADS TO MANY SPECIES BEING CAUGHT BESIDES TUNA. SWORDFISH, TURTLES, SEABIRDS, AND SHARKS ALL FALL VICTIM TO THESE BAITED HOOKS.

IN FACT, LONG-LINING IS A PRIMARY REASON MILLIONS OF SHARKS ARE KILLED EVERY YEAR.

4

AS YOU KNOW, OUR JOURNEY IN SEARCH OF A MASSIVE GREAT WHITE SHARK BEGINS HERE...

...IN THE COLORFUL TOWN OF GANSBAAI, 120 MILES SOUTHEAST OF CAPE TOWN, SOUTH AFRICA, A PLACE OF MYTHS, STORIES, AND LEGENDS.

VERY COOL.

I'LL FILL YOU BOTH IN ON THE DETAILS OF OUR EXPEDITION SHORTLY. RIGHT NOW, LET'S HOP IN MY JEEP AND DRIVE OVER TO THE HARBOR TO MEET THE CREW.

SOUNDS GOOD.

I'M CURIOUS, FABIEN. WHAT DOES "GANSBAAI" MEAN?

GOOSE BAY.

IT'S NAMED AFTER THE COLONIES OF EGYPTIAN GEESE THAT ONCE FLOUR-ISHED HERE. BECAUSE OF ITS NATURAL BEAUTY AND THE BOUNTY OF THE ENVIRONMENT, SOME PEOPLE BELIEVE THIS IS WHERE THE STORY OF THE GARDEN OF EDEN ORIGINATED, THE SACRED PLACE WHERE ADAM AND EVE LIVED. NOW THIS TOWN IS HOME TO ONE OF THE VERY FEW WORKING FISH-ING VILLAGES LEFT IN THE WESTERN CAPE OF SOUTH AFRICA. THE FISHING INDUSTRY, WHICH HAS A LONG HISTORY, DATES BACK TO THE 1800S. BEFORE THAT, SHEEP AND CATTLE FARMERS OCCUPIED THIS LAND. AND BEFORE THAT, THE FIRST EXPLORER SHIPS DOCKED HERE FOR FRESH FOOD AND WATER.

I WONDER WHAT LIFE MUST HAVE BEEN LIKE FOR THOSE EARLY EXPLORERS.

I'M SURE IT WAS DIFFICULT.

MORE THAN *150* WRECKS LIE ALONG THIS RUGGED COASTLINE...

...AT THE BOTTOM OF THE INDIAN OCEAN, A SILENT TESTIMONY TO THE PERILOUS SEA THOSE MARINERS ENCOUNTERED DURING THEIR VOYAGES AROUND SOUTH AFRICA. ONE SUCH SHIP IS THE HMS *BIRKENHEAD*, A FAMOUS TWO-MAST IRON-HULLED PADDLE-WHEEL SHIP BUILT FOR THE ROYAL NAVY. SHE WENT DOWN OFF GANSBAAI IN *1852*, SUPPOSEDLY WITH *3* TONS OF GOLD AND SILVER COINS...WHICH HAS NEVER BEEN FOUND.

THE SINKING OF THE HMS *BIRKENHEAD* WAS THE EARLIEST MARITIME DISASTER THAT USED THE CONCEPT OF "WOMEN AND CHILDREN FIRST" IN A SHIP'S EVACUATION PROCEDURE DURING A STATE OF EMERGENCY. TODAY, "WOMEN AND CHILDREN FIRST" IS STANDARD PROCEDURE FOR SINKING SHIPS.

THE CREAKING DOCK WE'RE STANDING ON IS PART OF KLEINBAAI.

LIFE AT THIS CHARMING HARBOR IS VERY MUCH ASSOCIATED WITH THE SEA AND FISHING INDUSTRY.

FIN CHASER Technical Data
Vessel Length: 33 feet
Width: 12 feet
Power: twin 200 hp Yamaha outboard motors
Features: spacious cabin, toilet/head and shower, large
        upper shark-viewing deck, pulpit, crane, and winch
Electronics: UHF radios, GPS (Global Positioning System),
        radar and navigation equipment, depth finder, echo
        sounder, SART (special rescue tracking device)
Medical and Safety: first aid kits, oxygen cylinders, life
        vests, fire extinguishers, emergency life raft

9

HOW OLD WOULD A SHARK LIKE THAT BE?

THAT'S A GOOD QUESTION.

I WOULD SAY A GREAT WHITE OVER 20 FEET...

...WOULD BE MORE THAN 50 YEARS OLD.

IT WOULD ALSO WEIGH WELL OVER 5,000 POUNDS.

IT'S LIKE THAT FAMOUS SHARK IN THE MOVIE JAWS.

WHILE TODAY'S GREAT WHITE SHARKS CAN GROW TO A LENGTH OF 20 OR MORE FEET, THEIR COUSIN, THE MEGALODON, COULD GROW TO 65 FEET! THEY WENT EXTINCT 1.5 MILLION YEARS AGO, WHICH IS PROBABLY A GOOD THING FOR HUMANS.

IF THIS SHARK IS MORE THAN 20 FEET, IT WOULD BREAK THE OFFICIAL RECORD, MAKING IT THE LARGEST LIVING GREAT WHITE SHARK EVER SEEN IN THE WORLD...

BUT UNLIKE THE CHARACTERS IN JAWS, WE'RE NOT HERE TO CATCH THE SHARK. IN FACT, THE GREAT WHITE SHARK IS ONE OF MANY SHARK SPECIES NOW PROTECTED IN SOUTH AFRICA AS WELL AS OTHER PLACES IN THE WORLD.

WE'LL BEGIN BY VISITING AN AREA BEST KNOWN FOR ITS LARGE CON- GREGATION OF GREAT WHITE SHARKS TO SEE IF WE CAN ENTICE THIS MEGA- SIZE SHARK TO COME IN FOR A CLOSER LOOK...

la: 34.6841
lo: 19.4148

WE JUST NEED TO BE SMART ABOUT THIS, MATES.

WE CAN'T LET OUR IMAGINATIONS GET THE BETTER OF US.

I AGREE, PAUL. WE MUST KEEP AN OPEN MIND IF WE WANT TO COLLECT IMPORTANT INFORMATION ABOUT THIS ELUSIVE ANIMAL TO HELP PROTECT IT.

AFTER ALL, GREAT WHITES, LIKE MANY OTHER SHARKS, ARE BECOMING INCREASINGLY ENDANGERED.

YOU'RE RIGHT ABOUT THAT, FABIEN. AS WE KNOW, SHARKS ARE BEING FISHED AT A RATE THAT'S FASTER THAN THEY CAN REPRODUCE.

ALREADY, SHARK POPULA- TIONS HAVE DECREASED, SOME AS MUCH AS 90 PERCENT IN JUST THE LAST 15 YEARS.

12

MANY ESTIMATE THAT MORE THAN *100* MILLION SHARKS ARE KILLED FOR THEIR FINS EVERY YEAR.

AND THAT MOST SHARK SPECIES WILL DISAPPEAR WITHIN *10* YEARS BECAUSE OF SHARK FISHING.

THAT'S HORRIBLE!

IT REALLY IS.

WITH SHARKS BEING THE LARGEST PREDATORY FISH ON EARTH AND AT THE TOP OF THE FOOD CHAIN, THESE APEX PREDATORS ARE VITAL TO THE OCEAN.

AMANDA'S RIGHT. BECAUSE SHARKS ROAM THE SEA CLEANSING IT OF THE DEAD, DISEASED, AND DECAYING, WE NEED SHARKS TO KEEP OUR OCEANS HEALTHY.

TO PUT IT ANOTHER WAY, A WORLD WITHOUT SHARKS IS A WORLD WITHOUT BALANCE.

16

17

NOW MIGHT BE A GOOD TIME TO FAMILIARIZE OURSELVES WITH THE DIFFERENT PARTS OF THE VESSEL.

PULPIT (raised platform off the bow)
BOW (front of boat)
GUNWALE (upper edge of a boat's side)
CABIN (inside the boat)
PORT (left side of the boat)
STARBOARD (right side of the boat)
HULL (body of the boat)
STERN (back or rear of the boat)
TRANSOM (the cross section of the stern)
CLEATS (metal fittings on which a rope can be fastened)
PROPELLER (rotates and powers a boat forward and backward)

THE LONGEST RECORDED FLIGHT FOR A FLYING FISH IS 45 SECONDS.

THAT'S EPIC. WHAT A LONG TIME FOR A FISH TO BE IN THE AIR!

FLYING FISH, WHICH EVOLVED 66 MILLION YEARS AGO, HAVE LONG, WING-LIKE FINS, SIMILAR TO BIRDS' WINGS, WITH WHICH THEY PROPEL THEMSELVES OUT OF THE WATER AND GLIDE IN THE AIR FOR A CONSIDERABLE DISTANCE. THIS IS THEIR NATURAL DEFENSE TO ELUDE PREDATORS SUCH AS SHARKS.

THIS IS WHAT I LOVE ABOUT THE OCEAN. IT HIDES SO MUCH MARINE LIFE, IT REALLY MAKES THESE TRIPS EXCITING.

YOU NEVER KNOW WHAT YOU'RE GOING TO ENCOUNTER AT SEA.

WHAT KIND OF DOLPHINS ARE THOSE?

THEY'RE BOTTLENOSE DOLPHINS, A MARINE MAMMAL THAT LIVES IN THESE WATERS.

THEY CAN REACH A LENGTH OF *12* FEET, BUT MOST ARE AROUND *6* TO *8* FEET.

LIKE THEIR NAME IMPLIES, BOTTLENOSE DOLPHINS HAVE SHORT, STUBBY BEAKS...

...WHILE THEIR THICK LAYER OF BLUBBER (OR FAT) HELPS MAINTAIN THEIR BODY HEAT AND PROTECTS THEM FROM PREDATORS SUCH AS SHARKS.

SOME DOLPHIN SPECIES FACE THE THREAT OF EXTINC-TION, OFTEN BECAUSE OF HUMAN BEHAVIOR. THE CHINESE RIVER DOLPHIN IS ONE SUCH DOLPHIN. IT WAS OFFICIALLY DECLARED EXTINCT IN *2006* DUE TO OVER-FISHING. OTHER DOLPHINS, LIKE THE BOTTLENOSE, ARE KILLED IN LARGE NUMBERS EVERY YEAR WHEN THEY GET TRAPPED IN FISHING NETS.

WHAT'S THAT HUGE TAIL OVER THERE?

WHY, THAT LARGE TAIL IN THE DISTANCE BELONGS TO THE SOUTHERN RIGHT WHALE.

LIKE MANY WHALES, THE SOUTHERN RIGHT WHALE IS A BALEEN WHALE.

THAT MEANS IT FILTERS LITTLE BITTY FOODS SUCH AS KRILL RATHER THAN USING TEETH LIKE A KILLER WHALE TO CONSUME LARGER PREY.

KRILL, SMALL SHRIMP-LIKE CRUSTACEANS ABOUT **2** INCHES IN LENGTH, ARE FOUND IN ALL OF THE WORLD'S OCEANS AND ARE A PRIMARY FOOD FOR BALEEN WHALES.

A SOUTHERN RIGHT WHALE IS EASY TO SPOT BECAUSE IT HAS A BIG, BROAD BACK AND A LONG, ARCHING MOUTH WITH ROUGH WHITE PATCHES OF SKIN ON ITS MEGA-SIZE HEAD.

THE SOUTHERN RIGHT WHALE GOT ITS NAME FROM AUSTRALIAN WHALERS IN THE *1800S*, WHO CLAIMED THESE WHALES WERE THE "RIGHT" WHALES TO CATCH BECAUSE OF THE LARGE AMOUNT OF WHALE OIL THAT COULD BE EXTRACTED FROM THEM AND USED TO ILLUMINATE LAMPS AND PROVIDE LUBRICATION FOR MACHINERY. WHALERS ALSO PREFERRED THE SOUTHERN RIGHT WHALE BECAUSE THEY WERE SLOW SWIMMERS, MAKING THEM AN EASY TARGET. FORTUNATELY, SOUTHERN RIGHT WHALES ARE NOW PROTECTED, WITH POPULATIONS ON THE RISE, MEANING MORE SIGHTINGS LIKE TODAY.

ANOTHER PROTECTED WHALE THAT CALLS SOUTH AFRICA HOME IS THE BRYDE'S WHALE.

LONG AND SLENDER WITH SHORT FINS AND A SMOKY BLUE COLOR, IT'S NAMED AFTER JOHAN BRYDE, WHO BUILT THE FIRST WHALING FACTORY IN SOUTH AFRICA, IN *1909*.

IT'S ALSO THE ONLY BALEEN WHALE THAT LIVES IN WARM WATER ALL YEAR ROUND.

IF YOU LOOK CLOSELY, YOU CAN SEE A NARROW CHANNEL OF WATER BETWEEN DYER ISLAND AND GEYSER ROCK.

THAT SHALLOW CHANNEL IS FAMOUSLY KNOWN AS SHARK ALLEY.

WE'RE CLOSE TO WHERE THOSE TUNA FISHERMEN SAW THAT GIANT SHARK.

WHAT MAKES SHARK ALLEY SO FAMOUS?

IT BEGINS WITH GEYSER ROCK...

...HOME TO MORE THAN 60,000 CAPE FUR SEALS, THE LARGEST SEAL COLONY ON THE AFRICAN COAST, AND A FAVORITE PREY OF GREAT WHITE SHARKS.

ACROSS THE CHANNEL IS DYER ISLAND, WHERE A COLONY OF 5,000 AFRICAN PENGUINS LIVES. THEY CAN ALSO MAKE FOR TASTY MEALS.

THE SEALS AND PENGUINS FROM THESE ISLANDS SWIM IN THE CHANNEL TO FEED, MAKING THEM QUITE VULNERABLE, WHICH IS WHY GREAT WHITE SHARKS PREFER THIS PLACE.

24

CHUM IS A SOUP-LIKE CONCOCTION, OFTEN USED TO ATTRACT SHARKS.

25

AND IF ALL GOES WELL, IT SHOULD FOLLOW YOUR CHUM TO ITS SOURCE, WHICH IS OUR BOAT.

WE'LL THEN KEEP IT OCCUPIED WITH THESE TUNA BAITS I'M TYING UP.

YELLOWFIN TUNA, NOTED FOR THEIR YELLOW FINS, ARE FOUND OFF THE SOUTHERN CAPE COAST IN SOUTH AFRICA.

AGAIN, WE'RE NOT TRYING TO CATCH THE SHARK, SO I'M NOT USING ANY HOOKS.

ALL WE WANT TO DO IS PULL THE BAITS AWAY AS THE SHARK MOVES IN TO BITE THEM.

THIS SHOULD KEEP IT ENTERTAINED FOR A WHILE, LIKE A CAT PLAYING WITH A BALL OF YARN.

THE LONGER WE CAN KEEP THE SHARK NEAR OUR BOAT, THE BETTER OPPORTUNITY WE'LL HAVE TO OBSERVE IT IN ITS NATURAL ENVIRONMENT.

BEFORE TAGGING A SPECIFIC SHARK THEY'RE INTERESTED IN, GREAT WHITE SHARK CONSERVANCY ORGANIZATIONS OFTEN FIRST OBSERVE THE SHARK FOR POPULATION STUDIES.

SOME SHARK LIVERS ARE UP TO **25** PERCENT OF THE ANIMAL'S BODY WEIGHT. SHARKS ALSO RELY ON THEIR HUGE, OILY LIVERS TO PROVIDE BUOYANCY. UNLIKE FISH, WHICH HAVE A GAS-FILLED SWIM BLADDER THAT KEEPS THEM AFLOAT IN THE WATER, SHARKS MUST SWIM CONSTANTLY OR THEY WILL SINK TO THE BOTTOM OF THE OCEAN AND DIE.

THE CAPE FUR SEAL IS THE LARGEST OF THE FUR SEAL SPECIES AND ONLY BREEDS IN SOUTH AFRICA. THE MALES (BULLS) CAN REACH A LENGTH OF 8 FEET, WHILE THE FEMALES (COWS) DON'T GROW MUCH MORE THAN 5 FEET. THEY ARE VERY ACTIVE AND SOCIAL IN THE WATER BUT TERRITORIAL ON LAND. THEIR MAIN PREDATOR IS THE GREAT WHITE SHARK.

WHAT ABOUT THE PENGUINS OVER THERE ON DYER ISLAND?

AFRICAN PENGUINS ARE FOUND ONLY IN SOUTHERN AFRICAN WATERS, PARTICULARLY ON DYER ISLAND, WHERE THEY FORAGE IN THE OPEN OCEAN FEEDING ON FISH AND SQUID, LIKE MANY OTHER MARINE ANIMALS. THEY ARE NOW CLASSIFIED AS ENDANGERED, AND HAVE A LIFE SPAN BETWEEN 10 AND 27 YEARS.

THEY TOO FALL PREY TO KILLER WHALES, AS WELL AS TO CAPE FUR SEALS AND GREAT WHITE SHARKS.

I CAN SEE WHY GREAT WHITE SHARKS LIKE TO HANG OUT HERE IN SHARK ALLEY.

PLENTY OF TUCKER, LIKE PAUL SAYS.

WHAT'S THAT BIG BIRD?

THAT'S A WANDERING ALBATROSS. THEY'RE ONE OF THE LARGEST BIRDS IN THE WORLD.

THEY ALSO HAVE THE LARGEST WING-SPAN OF ANY BIRD.

THE WANDERING ALBATROSS IS KNOWN TO EAT ALMOST ANYTHING IT COMES ACROSS AND WILL FOLLOW SHIPS IN THE HOPES OF FEEDING ON ITS SCRAPS OR GARBAGE OR IN THIS CASE, CHUM. THESE BIRDS ARE KNOWN FOR GORGING THEMSELVES WITH SO MUCH FOOD THAT THEY ARE UNABLE TO FLY AND MUST FLOAT ON THE WATER, MAKING THEM VULNERABLE TO CURIOUS SHARKS PATROLLING BELOW.

I READ THERE ARE MORE THAN 50 SPECIES OF OCEANGOING BIRDS THAT HAVE BEEN RECORDED IN THE WATERS AROUND SOUTH AFRICA, INCLUDING 16 OF THE WORLD'S 21 ALBATROSS SPECIES.

31

AND BECAUSE THERE ARE NO BOUND-ARIES OUT AT SEA, VARYING WINDS CAN CAUSE BIRDS TO TRAVEL FAR OFF THEIR NORMAL COURSE. IT'S NO SUR-PRISE WE'RE BEING TREATED TO THIS RARE VIEW OF THE WANDERING ALBATROSS.

WHAT OTHER BIRDS MIGHT WE SEE BESIDES THE ALBATROSS AND ALL THE GULLS?

TWO COMMON SEABIRDS OUT HERE ARE THE CAPE GANNET AND CAPE CORMORANT.

I THINK I SPOT SOME OVER THERE ON THE ROCK.

LIKE THE WANDERING ALBATROSS, CAPE GANNETS ARE COASTAL BIRDS THAT FEAST ON WHAT THE OCEAN PROVIDES, OFTEN PLUNGING DEEP UNDERWATER TO CATCH FISH. BECAUSE THEY LIVE SO CLOSE TOGETHER, THEY'RE OFTEN SEEN PECKING AT ONE ANOTHER WHILE TRYING TO MAKE SPACE FOR THEIR CLUMSY LANDINGS AND TAKEOFFS.

THE CAPE CORMORANT, MEANWHILE, IS A GLOSSY BLACK BIRD THAT ALSO FEEDS ON FISH AND OTHER MARINE CRITTERS BY DIVING BELOW AND SNARING FISH IN ITS SPECIALLY ADAPTED BILL, WHICH HELPS IT TO HUNT IN THE WATER.

CRIKEY, IT'S ANOTHER FIN!

WHERE'S THE FIN? I DON'T SEE IT!

RIGHT THERE, OFF THE PORT SIDE!

NOW, THAT'S THE FIN OF A GREAT WHITE SHARK!

THERE ARE NO GREAT WHITE SHARKS THAT LIVE AROUND DYER ISLAND AND GEYSER ROCK YEAR ROUND. THE SHARKS THAT COME HERE FOR A FEW WEEKS TO A MAXIMUM OF SEVERAL MONTHS ARE TRANSIENT SHARKS, MEANING THEY MIGRATE TO DIFFERENT PLACES THROUGHOUT THE YEAR.

THE SCIENTIFIC NAME OF THE GREAT WHITE SHARK IS CARCHARODON CARCHARIAS, WHICH MEANS "RAGGED TOOTH."

THE GREAT WHITE SHARK IS TORPEDO-SHAPED AND MADE UP OF THREE SECTIONS: THE HEAD, TRUNK, AND TAIL.

THE SKIN OF THE GREAT WHITE SHARK, LIKE MOST SHARKS, IS MADE UP OF SMALL TOOTH-LIKE SCALES CALLED DERMAL DENTICLES, WHICH MAKE THEIR SKIN FEEL ROUGH, LIKE SAND-PAPER.

THE SHARK'S SKIN IS ALSO PERFECTLY CAMOUFLAGED. FROM BELOW, THE SHARK'S WHITE BELLY BLENDS IN WITH THE SKY ABOVE, WHILE FROM ATOP THE WATER, THE SHARK'S GUNMETAL GRAY BACK IS ALMOST INVISIBLE AGAINST THE DARK OCEAN FLOOR BELOW. THIS IS BETTER KNOWN AS COUNTERSHADING, WHICH MAKES THEM DIFFICULT TO SEE IN THE WATER.

UNFORTUNATELY, SHARKS ARE OFTEN KILLED FOR THEIR SKIN, WHICH IS USED FOR VARIOUS LEATHER PRODUCTS LIKE WALLETS AND HANDBAGS, AS WELL AS SHAGREEN, A TYPE OF SANDPAPER.

DORSAL FINS
THESE FINS ALSO KEEP THE SHARK STABLE IN THE WATER, AND ARE THE FINS WE'RE MOST FAMILIAR WITH, SINCE THEY'RE OFTEN SEEN SLICING THROUGH THE WATER.

PECTORAL FINS
THESE FINS ALLOW THE SHARK TO LIFT AND STEER WHILE SWIMMING.

GILLS
THE GREAT WHITE SHARK HAS FIVE GILL OPENINGS ON EACH SIDE OF ITS HEAD, WHICH HELPS THE SHARK TO BREATHE. THE WATER RUSHES THROUGH THE SHARK'S MOUTH AND OVER THE GILLS AS OXYGEN IS EXTRACTED, AND THEN THE WATER EXITS THROUGH THE GILL SLITS ON EACH SIDE. THIS IS ANOTHER REASON WHY A SHARK MUST KEEP MOVING. SHOULD IT STOP, WATER WON'T ENTER THE MOUTH AND IT WILL STOP BREATHING AND DIE.

AMPULLAE OF LORENZINI
THESE ARE SENSORY CELLS AROUND THE SHARK'S HEAD THAT HELP THE SHARK DETECT PREY IN THE WATER.

EYES
THE GREAT WHITE SHARK HAS EXCEPTIONAL EYESIGHT, EVEN IN LOW LIGHT. IT ALSO HAS A SET OF EYE MUSCLES THAT CAN ROLL THE EYES BACK INTO ITS SOCKETS FOR PROTECTION, ESPECIALLY WHEN FEEDING OR ATTACKING PREY.

NOSTRILS
LIKE ITS EYESIGHT, THE GREAT WHITE SHARK'S SENSE OF SMELL IS EXCEPTIONAL.

MOUTH
THE GREAT WHITE SHARK HAS MULTIPLE ROWS OF TEETH, WHICH ARE CONSTANTLY REPLACED. THE LARGE UPPER TEETH ARE USED FOR TEARING, WHILE THE SMALLER LOWER TEETH ARE USED FOR GRIPPING. UNLIKE A HUMAN, THE GREAT WHITE SHARK DOESN'T CHEW ITS FOOD. INSTEAD, IT BITES ITS PREY AND SHAKES ITS HEAD FROM SIDE TO SIDE, TEARING OFF LARGE PIECES OF FLESH OR BLUBBER. THE GREAT WHITE CAN EAT ABOUT 30 POUNDS OF FLESH IN ONE BITE.

INSTEAD, A SHARK'S ENTIRE BODY IS MADE UP OF CARTILAGE, THE SAME TOUGH MATERIAL FOUND IN OUR NOSE AND EARS.

THIS ALLOWS THE SHARK TO BE LIGHTER AND MORE FLEXIBLE IN THE WATER, LIKE YOU'RE SEEING AS IT CIRCLES OUR BOAT.

GREAT WHITE SHARKS ARE TYPICALLY SOLITARY HUNTERS, SPENDING MOST OF THEIR LIVES ALONE, EXCEPT DURING MATING SEASON. THEY'RE ALSO ONE OF THE FEW SHARKS THAT LIKE TO INVESTIGATE THEIR PREY FIRST. THEY'LL LIFT THEIR HEADS ABOVE THE WATER AND GIVE A GOOD LOOK AROUND. THIS BEHAVIOR IS KNOWN AS SPY-HOPPING.

HE'S COMING TOWARD IT...

...HERE HE COMES...

HERE HE COMES!

41

SPOT STANDS FOR "SMART POSITION AND TEMPERATURE."

ONCE THE TAG IS SECURELY ANCHORED TO THE SHARK—IN THIS CASE, TO ITS DORSAL FIN—INFORMATION ABOUT THE SHARK'S WHEREABOUTS AND ITS MOVEMENTS, ALONG WITH MEASUREMENTS SUCH AS WATER TEMPERATURE AND ITS SWIMMING DEPTHS, ARE RELAYED TO A SATELLITE AND BACK TO THE RESEARCHERS AS SOON AS THE FIN BREAKS THE SURFACE OF THE WATER.

I'M SURE SOMEWHERE BACK AT A LAB IN GANSBAAI, MARINE BIOLOGISTS ARE RECEIVING INFORMATION ABOUT THIS SHARK RIGHT NOW, WHICH THEY'LL SHARE WITH OTHER SCIENTISTS AND THE PUBLIC.

HOW COOL IS THAT?

GREAT WHITE SHARKS HAVE BEEN TRACKED SWIMMING AT INCREDIBLE DEPTHS OF UP TO *3,900* FEET. THEY'LL DIVE THIS DEEP TO FEED IN WHAT IS CALLED THE "DEEP SCATTERING LAYER," WHERE THERE'S A DENSE POPULATION OF FISH AND SQUID.

BECAUSE WE WON'T BE ABLE TO SAFELY ATTACH A *SPOT* TAG TO OUR MONSTER-SIZE SHARK FROM THIS BOAT, WE WILL BE USING A *PSAT* TAG, WHICH STANDS FOR "POP-UP SATELLITE ARCHIVAL TAG." THIS TAG IS ANCHORED TO THE SHARK USING THE STEEL TAGGING HARPOON THAT AMANDA AND BELLA ASSEMBLED, WHICH WON'T HARM THE SHARK.

THE *PSAT* TAG, LIKE FABIEN MENTIONED, IS ANOTHER TYPE OF SATELLITE TRANSMITTER THAT WILL ALLOW US TO ANSWER QUESTIONS ABOUT THE SHARK'S MIGRATORY PATTERNS, FEEDING MOVEMENTS, DAILY HABITS, AND EVEN SURVIVAL, SHOULD THIS SHARK BE CAUGHT ON A LONGLINE OR NET AND BE RELEASED ALIVE.

THE COOL THING ABOUT *PSAT* TAGS IS THAT THEY DETACH FROM THE SHARK AT A SPECIFIC DATE AND TIME THAT WE PREPROGRAM INTO THE TAG.

THE TAG THEN FLOATS TO THE SURFACE AND UPLOADS THE DATA TO A LAND-BASED COMPUTER VIA A SATELLITE, JUST LIKE THE *SPOT* TAG.

THEN WE CAN ACCESS THE INFORMATION MANUALLY, ALLOWING US TO ANALYZE AND LEARN MORE ABOUT THE SHARK WE TAGGED.

THERE ARE MANY DIFFERENT TAGS USED TO TRACK AND STUDY SHARKS, BUT LIKE FABIEN SAID, WE'LL BE USING *PSAT* TAGS ON THIS MISSION.

GREAT WHITE SHARKS WILL MAKE FREQUENT MIGRATIONS, SOME JOURNEYS TAKING THEM MORE THAN *12,000* MILES.

WHAT WAS IT LIKE TO SEE A SHARK THAT BIG?

EXCITING, YET NERVE-RACKING AT THE SAME TIME.

OUR VESSEL WAS ONLY *23* FEET, SO IMAGINE A SHARK ALMOST AS LONG AS YOUR BOAT!

YOU THINK YOU'RE STARING AT A WHALE BECAUSE YOU CAN'T FATHOM A SHARK BEING THAT BIG. NOW YOU CAN SEE WHY THOSE TUNA FISHERMEN I TOLD YOU ABOUT WERE STARTLED WHEN THEY SAW THAT MONSTER-SIZE SHARK.

IT'S LIKE THAT CLASSIC SCENE FROM JAWS WHEN CHIEF BRODY, FRIGHT-ENED BY THE MASSIVE SHARK THAT SURFACED, BACKS INTO THE WHEEL-HOUSE AND INFORMS THE CAPTAIN, "YOU'RE GONNA NEED A BIGGER BOAT."

ANYWAY, OUR SHARK WASN'T AFRAID OF ANY-THING, AND WHY SHOULD SHE BE?

PROBLEM WAS, WHEN SHE TOOK OUR BAIT, JUST LIKE YOU SAW MOMENTS AGO WITH THE SMALLER SHARK, THE ROPE GOT CAUGHT BETWEEN HER TEETH LIKE A PIECE OF DENTAL FLOSS AND SHE PANICKED.

THERE ISN'T ANYTHING IN THE OCEAN THAT CONSI-DERS HER PREY.

SHE TRIED TO SWIM AWAY, BUT THE ROPE WAS TIED TO THE CLEAT, SO SHE BEGAN DRAGGING OUR BOAT WHILE THE CREW AND I ON DECK GOT DOUSED BY SPLASHING SEAWATER FROM HER POWERFUL TAIL.

FOR A MOMENT, I DID FEEL A LITTLE NERVOUS.

FORTUNATELY, THE ROPE MANAGED TO FREE ITSELF FROM THE SHARK'S MOUTH AND THE EXCITEMENT WAS OVER. WE NEVER SAW HER AGAIN.

IF THAT SHARK WAS 18 FEET, WHAT COULD A SHARK OVER 20 FEET DO?

A LOT OF DAMAGE IF SHE REALLY WANTED TO...BUT THEY'RE NOT OUT TO CAUSE TROUBLE.

THEY'RE JUST INVESTIGATING WHAT'S GOING ON.

REMEMBER, WE'RE THE ONES WHO ARE PUSHING THEIR BUTTONS AND GETTING THEM EXCITED BY TEASING THEM WITH CHUM AND TUNA.

WHEN WE'RE OUT HERE, WE ARE IN THEIR HOME. THEY'RE JUST DOING WHAT THEY NATURALLY DO, WHICH IS TO FEED AND REPRODUCE. IT'S WE WHO ARE ALTERING THEIR DAILY ROUTINE.

DAY 1: AUGUST 9, 2:47 PM

FOR THOSE OF YOU WHO HAVE NEVER ENTERED A SHARK CAGE AND GONE EYEBALL-TO-EYEBALL WITH A GREAT WHITE SHARK, NOW'S YOUR CHANCE.

IS THAT PLASTIC CAGE REALLY GOING TO PROTECT US FROM A GREAT WHITE SHARK?

DON'T WORRY. A GREAT WHITE SHARK CAN'T CRUSH A SHARK CAGE LIKE A SODA CAN.

THAT'S ONLY IN THE MOVIES. THE REALITY IS THIS CAGE IS CONSTRUCTED FROM THICK PLEXIGLASS AND IS VIRTUALLY INDESTRUCTIBLE. THE CAGE WILL ALSO FLOAT RIGHT NEXT TO THE BOAT FOR SAFETY.

A SHARK CAGE IS GENERALLY MADE FROM ALUMINUM AND STEEL MESH THAT'S MELDED TOGETHER. HOWEVER, NEW TECHNOLOGY IS NOW ALLOWING FOR OTHER MATERIALS TO BE USED, SUCH AS PLEXIGLASS. WITH A PLEXIGLASS CAGE, THERE AREN'T ANY METAL BARS TO OBSTRUCT ONE'S VIEW AND THERE AREN'T ANY SHARP EDGES ON WHICH A SHARK CAN INJURE ITSELF. MOST COUNTRIES HAVE REGULATIONS ON CAGE STRENGTH AND WHERE AND WHEN YOU CAN USE THEM. TYPICALLY, A SHARK CAGE WILL FIT TWO TO FOUR DIVERS AT A TIME.

IS SHARK CAGE DIVING ETHICAL? MARINE BIOLOGISTS HAVE BEEN TRACKING GREAT WHITE SHARKS IN GANSBAAI FOR MANY YEARS. THEIR STUDIES SHOW THAT SHARKS THAT ARRIVE IN SHARK ALLEY SPEND LESS TIME AROUND CAGE-DIVING BOATS, AS THEY PREFER TO FOCUS THEIR ATTENTION ON NATURAL PREY SUCH AS THE CAPE FUR SEALS AND ABUNDANT FISH SPECIES. IN ADDITION, THERE'S BEEN NO RESEARCH TO SUPPORT THE IDEA THAT WHITE SHARKS DISPLAY MORE AGGRESSION TOWARD HUMAN BEACH USERS, INCLUDING SURFERS, AFTER SUCH CAGE-DIVING AND CHUMMING ACTIVITIES.

OUR SEAL DECOY IS MADE FROM A MOLD TAKEN FROM A REAL SEAL. IT'S SIMPLY A FIBERGLASS SKIN COVERING A FOAM-RUBBER CORE.

WHY IS IT HARD ON THE OUTSIDE? AREN'T SEALS SUPPOSED TO BE SOFT?

THEY SURE ARE. BUT IF WE USED ALL FOAM AND RUBBER, THESE DECOYS WOULD GET EATEN BECAUSE THE TEXTURE WOULD RESEMBLE SEAL BLUBBER, AND WE DON'T WANT SHARKS EATING RUBBER. THIS FIBER-GLASS SHELL MAKES THE SHARK KNOW IT'S GOT A FAKE, AND IT WILL SPIT IT OUT.

THE DECOY LOOKS TOTALLY REAL.

AND IT WILL MOVE LIKE A REAL SEAL TOO.

THE TRICK IS KNOWING HOW TO MIMIC A SEAL IN THE WATER. LIKE A FISHING LURE, PRESENTATION AND TECHNIQUE ARE EVERYTHING IF YOU WANT THE SHARK TO FOLLOW AND BITE IT.

THAT'S WHAT OUR SEAL DECOY WILL REPRESENT... THAT ONE SEAL THAT'S VULNERABLE TO ATTACK.

STILL, THE HUNTING STRATEGY OF A GREAT WHITE SHARK IS FAR FROM A SURE THING.

INTERCEPTING A SWIMMING SEAL IS THE SHARK'S MOST DIFFICULT CATCH.

IT SEEMS 1 OUT OF 10 ATTEMPTS IS SUCCESSFUL.

DOES THAT MEAN SOME GREAT WHITES ARE CLEVER AND SOME ARE NOT SO CLEVER?

YOU COULD SAY THAT, MATE.

SOME GREAT WHITES WILL SMASH THE DECOY ON THE FIRST PASS WHILE ANOTHER SHARK MAY MAKE UP TO 8 OR 10 ATTEMPTS BEFORE SUCCESS-FULLY CATCHING IT.

WELL, LET'S GIVE IT A TRY AND SEE IF WE CAN'T ENTICE OUR GIANT SHARK.

IT'S SO LONG... ALMOST AS LONG AS OUR BOAT.

THEY CAN GROW UP TO 50 FEET IN LENGTH.

WHICH IS WHY OARFISH ARE OFTEN BELIEVED TO BE THE ORIGIN OF MANY SEA SERPENT LEGENDS.

OARFISH ARE LONG PELAGIC (OPEN OCEAN) FISH AND ONE OF THE MOST RARELY SEEN ANIMALS ON EARTH.

WHAT DO OARFISH EAT?

THEIR FAVORITE MEAL IS KRILL, BUT THEY WILL ALSO EAT SMALL JELLYFISH AND SQUID.

AND UNLIKE THE GREAT WHITE SHARK, WHICH HAS NO BONES, OARFISH ARE THE LONGEST BONY FISH IN THE SEA.

WILL THE SHARK FOLLOW THE SEAL FROM BEHIND LIKE THE OTHER SHARKS DID WITH OUR CHUM?

NOT NECESSARILY. WITH A MOVING SEAL, A GREAT WHITE WILL OFTEN BEGIN BY POSITIONING ITSELF IN THE CHANNEL WHERE THE SEALS SWIM TO AND FROM THE ISLAND.

THE SHARK WILL THEN HUG THE BOTTOM.

WHEN THE SEAL SWIMS OVERHEAD, THE SHARK WILL ROCKET UPWARD FROM BELOW IN LESS THAN 3 SECONDS AND TRY TO CATCH THE SEAL IN ITS MOUTH.

THAT DOESN'T GIVE THE SEAL MUCH TIME TO GET OUT OF THE WAY.

EXACTLY. IT'S THE ELEMENT OF SURPRISE.

AND SADLY FOR A REAL SEAL, IT DOESN'T STAND A CHANCE AFTER BEING HIT WITH SUCH FORCE BY A GREAT WHITE SHARK.

WOW!

HE GOT THE SEAL!

I CAN'T BELIEVE A SHARK THAT BIG CAN DO THAT!

THAT'S BECAUSE THE SHARK ROCKETED UP FROM BELOW, JUST LIKE PAUL EXPLAINED, AT A SPEED OF ABOUT 35 MILES AN HOUR, CARRYING ITS MOMENTUM BEYOND THE WATER'S SURFACE AND HIGH INTO THE AIR.

WHICH I'D SAY IS ABOUT 15 FEET HIGH.

IT'S STILL NOT OUR SHARK, BUT IT'S ALWAYS ASTONISHING TO WITNESS A GREAT WHITE SHARK BREACH.

AND IT CART-WHEELED, TOO!

THEY OFTEN CARTWHEEL AFTER THEY EXPLODE FROM THE WATER BECAUSE ALL OF THE ANIMAL'S MUSCLE MASS IS CONCENTRATED TOWARD ITS LARGE HEAD.

MOST PEOPLE ARE IMPRESSED WITH THE PREDATORY POWER OF THE GREAT WHITE, MORE SO THAN ANY OTHER SHARK.

EIGHT BREACHES AND STILL NO SIGN OF OUR MEGA SHARK.

MAYBE OUR SEAL IS TOO SMALL?

YOU MIGHT BE RIGHT, BELLA. TOMORROW MORNING LET'S TOW A LARGER SEAL.

MAYBE OUR SHARK IS LOOKING FOR A BIGGER MEAL.

BECAUSE AN ADULT SEAL MORE CLOSELY RESEMBLES A HUMAN THAN THE SMALL DECOY WE USED YESTERDAY, OUR FINDINGS MAY ALSO PROVIDE USEFUL INFORMATION THAT CAN REDUCE THE RISK OF ATTACKS AND HELP KEEP HUMANS SAFER IN THE WATER.

MY MATE'S RIGHT.

NO ONE KNOWS IF GREAT WHITE SHARKS PREFER SMALLER SEALS BECAUSE THEY'RE EASIER TO CAPTURE, OR BECAUSE THEY'RE LESS DANGEROUS TO THE SHARK.

BY OBSERVING THE DETAILS OF HOW THE SHARK APPROACHES THIS ADULT DECOY, WE WILL GAIN VALUABLE INSIGHT INTO THIS KEY QUESTION OF GREAT WHITE PREDATION STRATEGY.

WHAT IF THAT GIANT SHARK BITES YOU?

SHOULDN'T BE A PROBLEM.

ZZZIP

THE LARGEST CONFIRMED GREAT WHITE SHARK TOOTH MEASURES LESS THAN 3 INCHES LONG.

SHOULD THAT SHEILA SINK HER TEETH INTO MY BUM, HER TEETH WILL NEVER PENETRATE DEEP ENOUGH TO PUNCTURE ME.

WHILE THE PROTEC-TIVE CAGE PROTECTS YOU FROM THE SHARK'S BITE FORCE.

GOOD ON YA, MATE! THAT'S RIGHT.

AND THE SHARK WILL BE PROTECTED TOO. THE SOFT RUBBER AND FOAM WON'T HURT HER WHEN SHE BITES.

I STILL THINK YOU'RE CRAZY.

72

GUITARFISH, NAMED AFTER THEIR SHAPE, WHICH RESEMBLES A GUITAR, ARE CLOSELY RELATED TO RAYS AND HAVE A SHARK-LIKE TAIL. THERE ARE ABOUT 50 DIFFERENT SPECIES OF GUITARFISH WORLDWIDE. THEY CAN REACH A LENGTH OF 5 OR 6 FEET, ALTHOUGH THE GUITARFISH FOUND IN THE INDO-PACIFIC CAN REACH 10 FEET.

CUTTLEFISH, MEANWHILE, ARE RELATED TO THE SQUID AND OCTOPUS. A CUTTLEFISH HAS AN ELONGATED BODY AND TENTACLES AROUND ITS MOUTH. THERE ARE ABOUT 120 SPECIES OF CUTTLE-FISH, WHICH ARE A FAVORITE MEAL FOR SHARKS.

I THINK WE FOUND WHERE THAT TREASURE FROM THE HMS *BIRKEN-HEAD* ENDED UP.

LOOKS LIKE ONE OF THE BLOKES WAS TRY-ING TO MAKE OFF WITH THE LOOT DURING THE SHIP'S SINKING.

UNFORTUNATELY, HE DIDN'T MAKE IT VERY FAR.

SHE DOESN'T APPEAR TO BE SHOWING SIGNS OF AGGRESSION...

SHE IS PUFFING HER GILLS AND GAPING AT ME, BUT I BELIEVE THOSE ARE COMMUNICATION SIGNALS.

YES, THEY ARE. SHE'S TRYING TO TALK TO YOU!

SHE'S VERY CAUTIOUS, DESPITE HER ENORMOUS SIZE.

QUITE DIFFERENT FROM THE TYPICAL GREAT WHITE THAT LIKES TO LUNGE TOWARD DIVERS IN A CAGE.

SO WHY IS SHE NOT ATTACKING THE SUB?

GOOD QUESTION, BELLA.

I THINK THE SUB'S SUBSTANTIAL SIZE IS ONE REASON.

THE SUB IS LONG AND FAT AND LOOKS EXCEPTIONALLY ROBUST, LIKE A WELL-FED SHARK.

APPEARS SHE DOESN'T WANT TO TAKE ANY UNNECESSARY RISKS.

PRECISELY. I WOULD IMAGINE THAT ANIMALS THAT LIVED ON THE PLANET FOR OVER 400 MILLION YEARS ARE HERE BECAUSE THEY'RE SMART AND BECAUSE THEY'RE SURVIVORS.

SURVIVORS DON'T TAKE ON UNNECESSARY RISKS...AND ATTACKING ANOTHER BIG SHARK IS UNDERTAKING AN UNNECESSARY RISK.

I'VE NEVER SEEN A GREAT WHITE THIS BIG!

SHE'S SWIMMING RIGHT ALONGSIDE ME...I'D SAY SHE'S A GOOD 23 FEET IN LENGTH.

THAT'S ONE MASSIVE SHARK, MATE!

SURE IS. SHE'S NOW SWIMMING RIGHT IN FRONT OF ME... BECAUSE THERE'S NO ENGINE OR BUBBLES, THE SHARK THINKS I'M REAL TOO.

YOU STILL BE CAREFUL DOWN THERE, FABIEN.

90

SHARKS, ESPECIALLY A MASSIVE ONE LIKE OURS, WILL ALWAYS LIVE THE MAJORITY OF THEIR LIVES OUT OF THE RANGE OF HUMAN EYES, SO THERE'S MUCH WE'LL NEVER KNOW ABOUT THESE MAGNIFICENT CREATURES. BUT, THANKS TO THE CONTINUING INCREASE IN TECHNOLOGY AND INTEREST, WE ARE STARTING TO LEARN MORE AND MORE ABOUT THESE AMAZING ANIMALS.

AS A MATURE, PREGNANT FEMALE, SHE'S THE PERFECT CANDIDATE TO CARRY A TRANSMITTER.

MAYBE WE'LL FINALLY LEARN WHERE A MASSIVE GREAT WHITE SHARK LIKE HER WILL BEAR HER YOUNG, OR WHERE SHE MIGHT MIGRATE TO WHEN SHE LEAVES THE WATERS OFF SOUTH AFRICA. KNOWING HER PATTERNS SHOULD MAKE FOR GREAT SCIENTIFIC DISCOVERIES.

INTERESTED FOLKS, INCLUDING KIDS LIKE BELLA AND MARCUS, WILL NOW BE ABLE FOLLOW HER ON TWITTER AND TRACK HER MOVEMENTS ONLINE, THANKS TO THE SATELLITE TRANSMITTER WE ATTACHED.

DAY 4: AUGUST 12, 6:30 PM

A SHARK CONSERVANCY IS TYPICALLY A NON-PROFIT ORGANIZATION COMMITTED TO RAISING AWARENESS OF SHARKS, PARTICULARLY GREAT WHITE SHARKS, THROUGH SCIENCE AND EDUCATION.

BELLA

THIS HAS REALLY OPENED UP A WHOLE NEW VISTA INTO THE WHITE SHARK'S WORLD.

YOU CAN SAY THAT AGAIN.

SCIENTISTS BELIEVE SHARKS NAVIGATE USING VISUAL CLUES, SUCH AS THE LOCATION OF THE SUN OR MOON. BELLA SWAM AROUND DYER ISLAND THREE TIMES, TWICE AROUND GEYSER ROCK, AND IS NOW TRAVELING NORTHWEST TO CAPETOWN.

DURING OUR TIME SPENT WITH THE SHARK, WHICH WE NAMED BELLA, WE WITNESSED HER BEAUTY AND MAG-NIFICENCE.

WE WERE ALSO FORTUNATE ENOUGH TO TAG HER SO WE CAN SHARE HER INFORMATION WITH YOU AND THE REST OF THE WORLD, ALL IN THE HOPES OF INSPIRING PEOPLE TO ADVOCATE FOR HER SURVIVAL.

I KNOW THE SHARK HAS BEEN LABELED AS A BLOODTHIRSTY SEA MONSTER AND A HUMAN DEVOURER, BUT IT DOES KILL PEOPLE.

YES, BUT ON AVERAGE, THE SHARK KILLS ONLY A HANDFUL OF HUMANS A YEAR, OFTEN ACCIDENTALLY, WHILE HUMANS KILL *100* MILLION SHARKS A YEAR, OFTEN INTENTIONALLY.

HUMANS KILLED BY SHARKS

SHARKS KILLED BY HUMANS

I AGREE WE DO MORE HARM TO THE SHARK THAN THE SHARK DOES TO US.

WHAT MANY PEOPLE DON'T KNOW IS THAT SHARKS ARE A VITAL ANIMAL TO OUR WORLD'S ECOSYSTEM, AND IF THE DECLINE IS NOT CONTROLLED, WE COULD BE FACING DEVASTATING PROBLEMS IN YEARS TO COME.

The authors would like to personally thank:

Illustrator Joe St.Pierre and agent Gail Thurm

Paul Zemitzsch and Explore Green

Craig Ferreira, white-shark-expeditioner
and researcher extraordinaire

Literary agents Sharlene Martin and Clelia Gore
of Martin Literary Management

Karen Wojtyla of Margaret K. McElderry Books

Marcus Kloss and Isabella Osseiran

Joe St.Pierre wishes to thank
Sonya Pelletier and Kael Arbon
for their coloring assistance.

FABIEN COUSTEAU is the grandson of famed sea explorer Jacques Cousteau and a third generation ocean explorer and filmmaker. He has worked with National Geographic, Discovery, PBS, and CBS to produce ocean exploration documentaries and continues to produce environmentally oriented content for schools, books, magazines, and newspapers. Learn more about his work at fabiencousteauolc.org.

JAMES O. FRAIOLI is a published author of twenty-five books and an award-winning filmmaker. He has traveled the globe alongside experienced guides, naturalists, and scientists, and has spent considerable time exploring and writing about the outdoors. He has served on the board of directors for the Seattle Aquarium and works with many environmental organizations. Learn more about his work at vesperentertainment.com.

JOE ST.PIERRE has illustrated for Marvel and DC Comics, and has the distinction of penciling the most #1 issues featuring Spider-Man and the Spider-Man family. Joe also works in the fields of intellectual property design, commercial illustration, and storyboards for animation and video games. Joe's publishing company, Astronaut Ink, highlights his creator-owned properties: the award-winning Megahurtz, Bold Blood, and New Zodiax. See his work at astronautink.com.